CRAFTY
Detectives

Nick Huckleberry Beak

Gareth Stevens Publishing
A WORLD ALMANAC EDUCATION GROUP COMPANY

The original publishers would like to thank the following children for modeling for this book: Steve Jason Aristizabal, Rula Awad, Nadia el-Ayadi, Nicola Game, Kevin Lake, Isaac John Lewis, Laura Harris-Stewart, Pedro Henrique Queiroz, Jamie Rosso, and Nida Sayeed. Thanks also to their parents and Hampden Gurney School.

The author would like to thank John Freeman (for keeping him sane during the photo shoot) and, also, his dad and Barbara and Mike for helping with the ideas.

For a free color catalog describing Gareth Stevens' list of high-quality books and multimedia programs, call 1-800-542-2595 (USA) or 1-800-461-9120 (Canada). Gareth Stevens Publishing's Fax: (414) 225-0377.

Library of Congress Cataloging-in-Publication Data

Beak, Nick Huckleberry.
    Crafty detectives / by Nick Huckleberry Beak.
      p. cm. — (Crafty kids)
    Includes bibliographical references and index.
    Summary: Describes what you need to know to be a detective, discussing how to collect information, send messages, and use disguises.
    ISBN 0-8368-2501-2 (lib. bdg.)
    1. Detectives—Juvenile literature. 2. Criminal investigation—Juvenile literature. 3. Police—Juvenile literature. [1. Detectives. 2. Police. 3. Criminal investigation.] I. Title. II. Series.
HV7922.B43   2000
363.25—dc21   99-041544

This North American edition first published in 2000 by
Gareth Stevens Publishing
A World Almanac Education Group Company
1555 North RiverCenter Drive, Suite 201
Milwaukee, WI 53212 USA

Original edition © 1997 by Anness Publishing Limited. First published in 1997 by Lorenz Books, an imprint of Anness Publishing Limited, New York, New York. This U.S. edition © 2000 by Gareth Stevens, Inc. Additional end matter © 2000 by Gareth Stevens, Inc.

Editors: Sam Batra, Lyn Coutts
Photographer: John Freeman
Designer: Michael R. Carter
Gareth Stevens series editor: Dorothy L. Gibbs
Editorial assistant: Diane Laska-Swanke

Printed in Mexico

1 2 3 4 5 6 7 8 9 04 03 02 01 00

Introduction

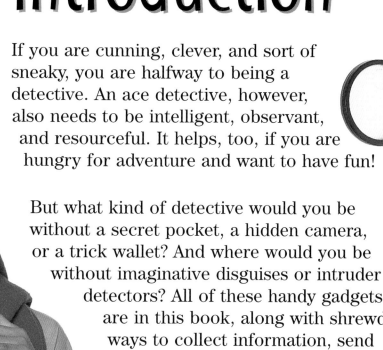

If you are cunning, clever, and sort of sneaky, you are halfway to being a detective. An ace detective, however, also needs to be intelligent, observant, and resourceful. It helps, too, if you are hungry for adventure and want to have fun!

But what kind of detective would you be without a secret pocket, a hidden camera, or a trick wallet? And where would you be without imaginative disguises or intruder detectors? All of these handy gadgets are in this book, along with shrewd ways to collect information, send confidential messages, and keep your "private eye" on things. You will also find out how to put together a basic detective's kit.

WARNING! Keep this book safe. Do not let it fall into the wrong hands. Good luck, Super Sleuth!

Nick Huckleberry Beak

Contents

GETTING STARTED

DETECTIVE FUN

Materials

Thick book

Aluminum foil

Brown wrapping paper

Flashlight

Paper bag

Mirrors

Playing cards

Lemon

ALUMINUM FOIL
You will need a small amount of foil to complete an electrical circuit for the "Electrical Trap" project.

BATTERY HOLDER
You can find plastic cases for batteries at stores that sell electrical supplies. For the "Electrical Trap" project, you will need a holder for two AA batteries.

BROWN WRAPPING PAPER
This heavy paper is available in sheets or rolls at stores that sell stationery or art supplies.

CRUNCHY CEREAL
For the "Noisy Alarms" project, you will need breakfast cereal that is crisp enough to make a noise when it is stepped on.

INK PAD
A black ink pad is best for the "Taking Fingerprints" project in this book. Keeping the lid on the ink pad closed will keep the pad moist.

MAGNIFYING GLASS
A magnifying glass makes fine details easier to see. A glass, rather than plastic, lens is best. Keep this tool in a fabric pouch to protect the lens.

CARBON PAPER
One side of carbon paper is coated with ink, the other is not. Place the inky side down on a sheet of plain paper to make a copy of whatever you write or draw on paper placed on top of the carbon paper.

FLASHLIGHT
For the projects in this book, you need only a small, plastic flashlight. Just remember to put batteries in it!

FLASHLIGHT BULB AND BASE
In addition to a regular flashlight, you will need just a flashlight bulb with a base. These items are easy to find at stores that sell electrical supplies, and they are not very expensive.

PLASTER OF PARIS
To use this white powder, mix it with water, following the instructions on the package. You will find it at art supply stores and craft shops.

PLASTIC-COATED ELECTRICAL WIRE
The fine strands of copper wire inside the plastic casing conduct electricity. Always have an adult help you cut and strip the wire. It is available in rolls at stores that sell electrical supplies.

MIRRORS
You will need four or five pocket-size mirrors to make all the projects in this book. The best mirrors to use are those mounted in a plastic frame with a plastic back.

PICTURE POSTCARD
For the project in this book, you can recycle an old picture postcard or cut the picture off a greeting card.

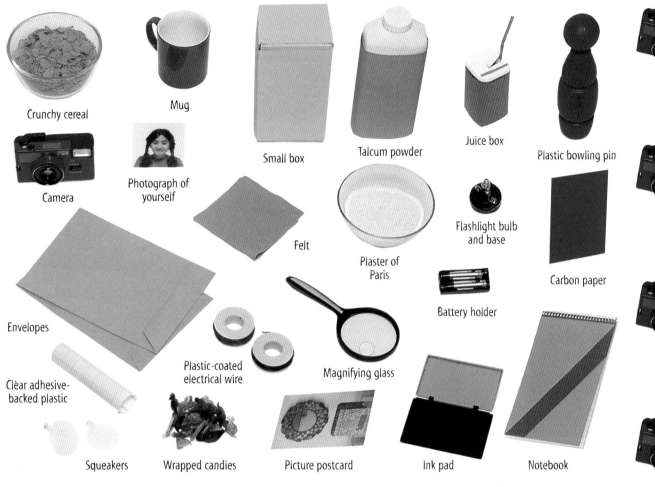

Crunchy cereal

Mug

Small box

Talcum powder

Juice box

Plastic bowling pin

Camera

Photograph of yourself

Felt

Plaster of Paris

Flashlight bulb and base

Carbon paper

Envelopes

Battery holder

Clear adhesive-backed plastic

Plastic-coated electrical wire

Magnifying glass

Squeakers

Wrapped candies

Picture postcard

Ink pad

Notebook

CLEAR ADHESIVE-BACKED PLASTIC

When its protective backing is peeled off, this clear plastic will stick to almost any surface. You can find it at variety and stationery stores.

FELT

Felt is a fabric that can be cut easily and does not fray. It comes in many bright colors.

CAMERA

You can use either a pocket-size camera or a disposable one.

PHOTOGRAPH OF YOURSELF

You will need a passport-size head-and-shoulders photograph of yourself to make your identification card. Be sure to ask permission before you cut up a family photograph.

SQUEAKERS

These hollow plastic disks that squeak when they are pressed are used to make stuffed toys. You can find them at stores that sell craft supplies.

TALCUM POWDER

You probably have a container of this sweet-smelling powder in your bathroom at home, but be sure to ask permission before you borrow it.

7

Equipment

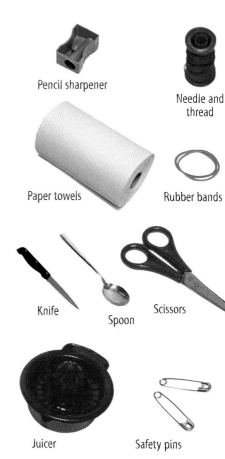

Pencil sharpener

Needle and thread

Paper towels

Rubber bands

Knife   Spoon   Scissors

Juicer   Safety pins

COLORED AND WHITE CARDBOARD AND PAPER

For the projects in this book, you will need pieces of cardboard and sheets of paper in both plain white and in colors. You can use either thin or stiff cardboard for most of the projects.

CRAYON

A crayon is perfect for shading large areas without making any impressions, or dents, in the paper like a pencil or pen would. Choose a strong, bright color for the "Seeing the Unseen" project.

JUICER

This kitchen utensil can be used to squeeze the juice out of the lemon for the "Invisible Writing" project. To use the juicer, press half of the lemon onto the ridged dome and twist the lemon back and forth. The juice will collect in the bowl around the dome.

TAPE

Both clear, or transparent, tape and electrical tape are needed for the projects in this book. Electrical tape is much stronger than transparent tape. It is available in many colors and widths at hardware stores and electrical supply stores.

PAINTBRUSHES

You will need both a clean, fine paintbrush and a large, soft paint-brush for projects in this book. The large brush has many more bristles than a normal paintbrush, and the bristles are much softer. You can buy one at a craft shop or at a stationery or hardware store.

PAPER TOWELS

These disposable towels are handy for wiping your hands and cleaning surfaces after completing projects.

RUBBER BANDS

You probably have rubber bands you can use right in your own home. If not, you can buy packages of them, in a variety of sizes, at office supply stores or even at supermarkets.

SCREWDRIVER

For the "Electrical Trap" project, you will need a small screwdriver with either a straight head or a Phillips head, depending on the kind of screws in the flashlight bulb base and the battery holder you will be using. Always be very careful when you are using a screwdriver (The head is sharp!) and always use a screwdriver that has an insulated handle.

KNIFE

You will need a sharp knife to cut a lemon in half for the "Invisible Writing" project. Ask an adult to help you use the knife.

NEEDLE AND THREAD

A regular sewing needle and plain thread are all you need for these projects. Try to match the color of the thread to the color of the material you are sewing.

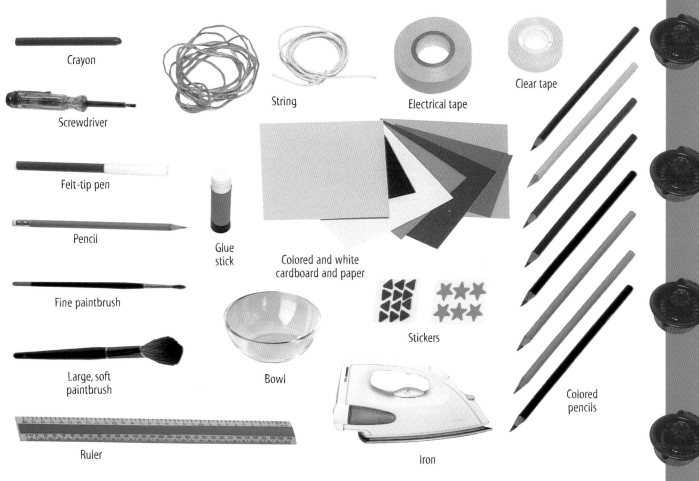

Crayon

Screwdriver

Felt-tip pen

Pencil

Fine paintbrush

Large, soft paintbrush

Ruler

String

Glue stick

Colored and white cardboard and paper

Bowl

Electrical tape

Clear tape

Stickers

Iron

Colored pencils

SAFETY PINS

Use medium or large safety pins for the projects in this book, but be very careful when using them. Safety pins have sharp points, and, even through they have safety catches, they can pop open unexpectedly.

STRING

You can use either plain or colored string, just be sure you have plenty of it.

BOWL AND SPOON

You will need a bowl and a spoon to mix plaster of Paris. Using old utensils is best because the hardened plaster is sometimes hard to remove.

IRON

You will need an electric iron for the "Invisible Writing" project. Ask an adult to plug it in and do the ironing. Even set at its coolest temperature, an iron can cause serious burns.

GLUE STICK

Glue for paper is clean and easy to use in stick form, but you can also use white or craft glue in squeeze bottles for these projects.

STICKERS

Adhesive-backed stickers are sold in sheets or rolls in most toy stores or at stores that sell stationery supplies. You can use stickers in plain colors or try shiny metallic ones.

Detective's Office

When not on surveillance or gathering evidence, a good detective is in the office, planning strategies for solving mysteries, making specialized equipment, and organizing vital pieces of evidence. To do his or her job, the detective's office must be well equipped and extremely secure.

Must-have office items include a notebook for recording information, separate files for different cases, and lots of pencils and pens.

A detective also needs a telephone to call contacts for information and to get calls from clients about their cases. A telephone can save a detective a lot of tiring legwork, but try not to use the telephone all the time — other members of your family might not appreciate it. Be a courteous detective by asking permission before using the telephone and by making sure that others have a chance to use it, too.

Detective's Kit

A good detective is always prepared for urgent jobs, so keep all your detective equipment handy in a sturdy backpack. A basic detective's kit consists of a notebook; a pencil; a magnifying glass; some plastic bags for storing physical evidence, such as an empty candy wrapper that might be covered with fingerprints; disposable plastic gloves for handling evidence; adhesive labels for tagging evidence; and a camera loaded with film. For special jobs, you might also need a flashlight and a pocket-size mirror.

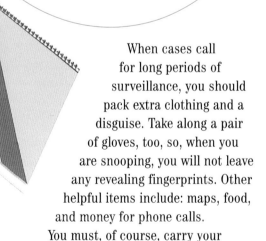

When cases call for long periods of surveillance, you should pack extra clothing and a disguise. Take along a pair of gloves, too, so, when you are snooping, you will not leave any revealing fingerprints. Other helpful items include: maps, food, and money for phone calls.

You must, of course, carry your badge and identification (ID) card at all times, and, before going on a case, tell an adult where you will be. To make surveillance jobs easier, detectives usually work in pairs or small teams. Be sure to tell an adult with whom you will be working.

All about Disguise

A detective has to be a master of quick disguises, but how — without carrying around a suitcaseful of outfits?

Disguise is easy! All you need are a change of clothes, a few simple props, and a little acting ability. To change, for example, from a streetwise detective to a corporate executive, wear a shirt and tie under your sweater or sweatshirt, put a pair of glasses in your pocket, and stash a suit coat, a briefcase, and a toy mobile phone in your backpack. To make the transformation, whip off your sweater, put on the suit coat and glasses, and hide your sweater and backpack inside the briefcase. Then act like an executive by talking on the mobile phone.

Useful items to collect for disguises are hats, glasses, and scarfs, which can be used to conceal the lower half of your face. If you are working on a case for which secrecy is particularly essential, buy a beard or a wig at a costume shop or a toy store. These items are inexpensive, and they can fool everyone — even your family!

Surveillance Skills

Watching a suspect or a particular place for a long period of time without being detected takes a lot of skill. There are two effective ways to keep from being seen: either hide under cover or try to blend in so you will not be noticed.

If there is something for you to hide behind, use it! It does not matter what it is — a wooden fence, a mailbox, trees, or even a crowd of people — as long as you can easily see your suspect without him or her seeing you.

Blending in with your surroundings is a little more difficult, but disguises and simple props come in handy. If, for example, you are watching a suspect in a shopping mall, load yourself up with shopping bags and pretend to be studying a shopping list. If your suspect is in a park, blend in by reading a newspaper or a book and listening to music. If you hold the newspaper or book up to your face, it will help hide your identity.

Perhaps the hardest surveillance job is watching someone in your own home. Brothers and sisters sometimes act crazy if you even so much as look at them. Your best cover at home is under a bed, in a closet, or behind a large piece of furniture.

If you have to be a super sleuth in home territory, keep in mind that you probably will not win any popularity contests. Always be considerate and never invade anyone's privacy — it could cost you your detective's badge and ID card!

Badge and ID Card

Making a detective's badge and ID card is a super sleuth's first assignment. Always keep them with you for identification and for getting into places that are off-limits to others. To make your badge and ID card look official, give yourself a code number and write it on both the badge and the card.

YOU WILL NEED
- Compass
- Ruler
- Colored cardboard
- Scissors
- Stickers
- Colored pencils
- Safety pin
- Clear tape
- Glue stick
- Photograph of yourself
- Felt-tip pen
- Clear adhesive-backed plastic

1 **Make a badge**: With a compass, draw a 2½-inch- (6-centimeter-) diameter circle on colored cardboard and cut it out. You could also make the badge triangular, rectangular, or even octagonal, if you prefer.

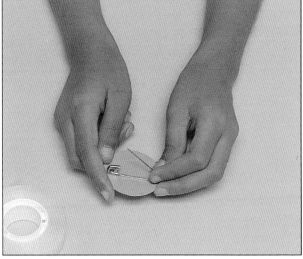

2 Decorate the front of the badge with colorful stickers or draw on your own designs with colored pencils. Carefully attach the safety pin to the back of the badge with pieces of clear tape.

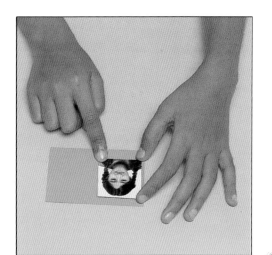

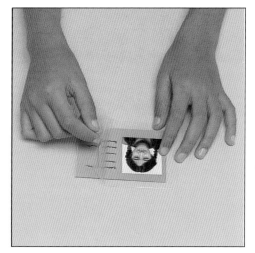

1 **Make an ID card:** Cut a rectangle, 4 inches (10 cm) by 2½ inches (6 cm), out of colored cardboard. Use a glue stick to attach your photograph on one side of the card (as shown). Alongside the photograph, write in, with a felt-tip pen, your name, age, rank, code number, height, eye and hair color, and favorite cookie.

2 Cut a piece of adhesive-backed plastic, making it slightly larger than the ID card. Peel off the protective backing and place the plastic, sticky side down, on the front of the ID card. Snip off the corners of the plastic, then fold the plastic over the edges of the card, sticking it to the back for a professional-looking finish.

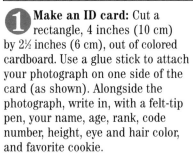

SAFETY TIP

Be careful when you are taping the safety pin to your badge or pinning the badge onto your T-shirt. You do not want to get hurt in the line of duty.

Dusting for Fingerprints

Because every person has unique fingerprints, all a detective has to do is match a fingerprint found at the scene of a crime to one in his or her files. When an identical fingerprint is found, Super Sleuth will know the name of the culprit. Getting good, clear fingerprints takes lots of practice, so leave no surface undusted!

YOU WILL NEED
- Mug
- Talcum powder
- Large, soft paintbrush
- Clear tape
- Black cardboard
- Magnifying glass
- Light colored pencil

1 Wash and dry a mug to remove any existing fingerprints. Then, without touching the mug yourself, ask a friend to hold the mug firmly by its sides and set it down on a table. Sprinkle talcum powder over one side of the mug until it is covered.

2 Use a large, soft paintbrush to gently dust most of the talcum powder off the mug. Do not try to blow the talcum off the mug because the moisture in your breath will make the powder stick even where there are no fingerprints.

3 Keep brushing gently until you find a fingerprint covered with a fine layer of talcum powder. Brush around the fingerprint to remove all excess talcum powder, handling the mug carefully so you will not smudge the fingerprint.

4 To make a permanent record of the fingerprint for your evidence files, press a piece of clear tape onto the mug over the fingerprint. When you peel off the tape, the fingerprint will come with it. Sneaky and clever at the same time!

5 Stick the tape onto black cardboard. The white fingerprint will show clearly on black so you can examine it with a magnifying glass. Write the name of the fingerprint's owner on the back of the cardboard with a light colored pencil.

HANDY HINT

The best places to dust for fingerprints are doorknobs, tabletops, stair railings, and the handles of cups and mugs. It is much easier to get a clear and complete fingerprint from a smooth surface.

Taking Fingerprints

Start by taking your own fingerprints and be prepared to get your fingers dirty! After you master the art of taking your own prints, create a file of fingerprints belonging to friends and family members. For each set of fingerprints, you will need cutouts of both a right and a left hand glued onto cardboard. Be sure to label each set of fingerprints with the name of its owner.

YOU WILL NEED
- Colored and white cardboard
- Pencil
- Scissors
- Glue stick
- Ink pad
- Paper towels

1 Place your right hand on colored cardboard and draw around it with a pencil. Your hand should be flat against the cardboard with fingers spread. Repeat this step with your left hand, using cardboard of a different color.

2 Cut out both hand shapes and use a glue stick to attach them to a piece of white cardboard (as shown, opposite). Leave enough space above the fingers to add your fingerprints.

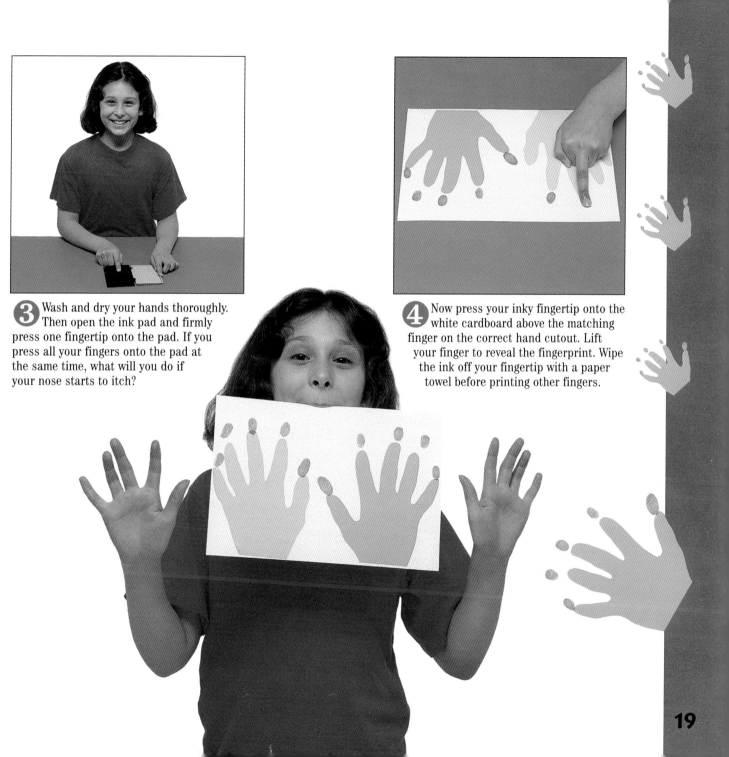

3 Wash and dry your hands thoroughly. Then open the ink pad and firmly press one fingertip onto the pad. If you press all your fingers onto the pad at the same time, what will you do if your nose starts to itch?

4 Now press your inky fingertip onto the white cardboard above the matching finger on the correct hand cutout. Lift your finger to reveal the fingerprint. Wipe the ink off your fingertip with a paper towel before printing other fingers.

Seeing the Unseen

When a piece of written information is whisked away before a detective's very eyes, that detective has to get sneaky! Here are two techniques for seeing the unseen and reading messages you were never intended to read. If you carry out these instructions to the letter, the message writer will never know what you have done — unless *you* spill the beans!

YOU WILL NEED
- Notebook
- Crayon
- Scissors
- Carbon paper

WARNING!
You are in grave danger if you get caught in the act of spying. You might have to end your career as a detective!

1 Finding out what was written on a page torn out of a notebook is as easy as coloring. The important thing is to get your hands on the notebook as quickly as possible.

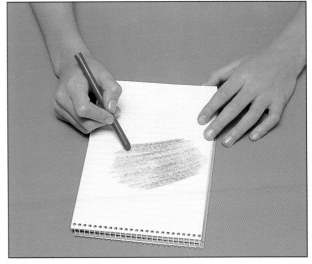

2 Rub a crayon gently over the top page of the notebook. The slight impressions made by the writing on the torn-off page will remain uncolored. This technique will not work, however, if the writing tool was a felt-tip pen.

1 To intercept a message as it is written, cut a sheet of carbon paper so it is smaller than the pages of the notebook. Turn over a few pages of the notebook and insert the carbon paper with the inky side down — then wait!

2 After the message has been written, and the person is out of sight, turn over the top pages of the notebook and remove the carbon paper. A carbon copy of the message will appear on the page beneath it.

HANDY HINT

There is one other way to read something not intended for your eyes. You could sneak a peek over the writer's shoulder.

Making a Plaster Cast

The villain left no fingerprints, but there are handprints in the sand. The only way to capture this vital piece of evidence is to make a plaster cast. It is a messy job, but someone has to do it! This project will give you some off-case plaster-casting practice.

YOU WILL NEED
- Sand (moist sand works best)
- Scissors
- Cardboard
- Clear tape
- Plaster of Paris
- Bowl
- Pitcher of water
- Old spoon
- Large, soft paintbrush

1 Pile sand on a covered work surface and gently flatten out the pile a little. With fingers spread, firmly press one hand into the sand. When you have made a clear print, take your hand out of the sand.

2 Cut a piece of cardboard into a strip 25 inches (63.5 cm) long and 2½ inches (6 cm) wide. Tape the ends of the strip together to form a ring and add more tape to seal the seam. Place the ring around the handprint and push it into the sand.

3 Make plaster of Paris by following the instructions on the package. You will need a bowl, a pitcher of water, and an old spoon. To make really good plaster of Paris, stir the mixture constantly and work quickly.

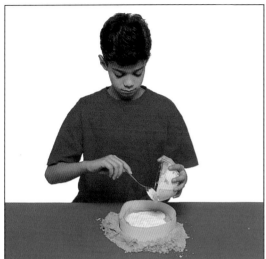

4 When the plaster mixture has a smooth, creamy consistency, pour it over your handprint. Use a spoon to ease the mixture gently into all the nooks and crannies. Pour on enough plaster to cover the sand evenly. To give the plaster cast a neat finish, spread the mixture up against the cardboard ring.

5 Most plaster of Paris mixtures harden in five to ten minutes, but the amount of time varies according to the thickness of the cast. When the plaster has hardened, remove the cardboard ring and lift up the cast. After brushing off any loose sand with a large, soft paintbrush, there is only one thing left to do — clean up the mess!

Peek-a-Book

The Peek-a-Book lets you keep an eye on someone or something without being detected. Lots of tiny holes in the front cover and a hidden window in the back cover of this fake book let you secretly watch what is happening. No one will suspect a thing!

YOU WILL NEED
- Colored cardboard
- Clear tape
- Paper
- Scissors
- Safety pin
- Pencil
- Ruler

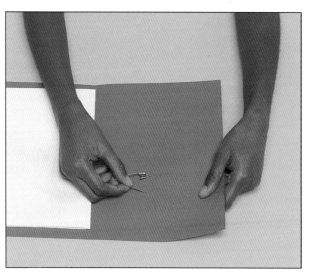

1 Fold a piece of colored cardboard in half. Tape one edge of a sheet of paper along the fold and trim it to fit. With a safety pin, poke lots of holes, close together, into the front of your "book," 2 inches (5 cm) from the top.

2 Hold the fake book up to your face with the pinholes at eye level. Pretend to be reading while you secretly watch a suspect. Your identity will be safe. No one will notice the tiny holes in the cover of your book.

3 Turn over the sheet of paper in your Peek-a-Book and, on the inside back cover, 3 inches (7.5 cm) below the top edge, draw a 2-inch (5-cm) by 1-inch (2.5-cm) rectangle and cut it out to make a window.

4 Use cardboard the same color as your book to make a rectangle that is slightly larger than the window cut into the back cover. Place this rectangle over the window and tape it down along one edge to make a flap.

5 To get a clearer view of a suspect, all you have to do is turn over the sheet of paper in your book and lift up the cardboard flap. Remember that the open window can be easily noticed, so take a fast peek, then quickly close the flap.

HANDY HINT

To disguise the window, cut a large picture of a face out of a magazine. Glue the face to the outside back cover of your book with one of the eyes positioned over the window. Cut out the eye and glue it to the back of the window flap. When the flap is closed, the picture of the face is complete. When the flap is open, your own eye will complete the picture!

Powerful Periscope

With this powerful periscope, you will be able to see over tall fences and into high windows without using a ladder or climbing a tree. You will even be able to see around corners. How does it work? With mirrors, of course! The best mirrors to use are rectangular, pocket-size mirrors that have a plastic frame and a plastic backing.

YOU WILL NEED
- Pencil
- Cardboard
- Ruler
- Two pocket-size mirrors
- Scissors
- Electrical tape
- Glue stick

WARNING!
Never use your periscope to look at the Sun. You will damage your eyes!

1 Draw five columns on a piece of cardboard. Make each column 16 inches (40.5 cm) long and a little wider than the mirrors. Number the columns (the sides of the periscope) one to five. Cut off any excess cardboard.

2 Draw and cut out a square near the top of side two. Make the square slightly narrower than the width of the column. Cut out another square at the bottom of side four.

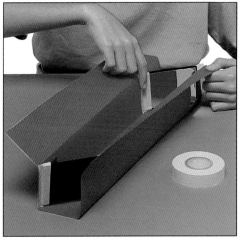

3 Fold the cardboard along each pencil line between the columns. Place one mirror, with the mirror side down, so it covers the opening in side two. Tape the mirror in place along the top edge. Place the other mirror, with the mirror side down, over the opening in side four and tape it in place along the bottom edge. Now this project gets tricky! Tape the bottom edge of the side two mirror to side four. The mirror will be angled facing downward. Next, tape the top edge of the side four mirror to side two.

4 Be sure the mirrors are securely taped into position. Then, fold side five over side one, glue it in place, and tape down the seam. Your powerful periscope is ready for action!

5 To use the periscope, look through the bottom opening with one eye. The top mirror will reflect whatever is in view onto the mirror at the bottom.

HANDY HINT

Getting the mirrors positioned at the right angles, so the periscope actually works, is tricky. It might be necessary to adjust the length of the periscope and the size of the openings in sides two and four.

Mystifying Map

This mystifying map is a very clever detective trick. The map is easy to make, but only those who know the secret folding technique will be able to use it. Anyone else who tries to follow the map's false directions will end up going around in circles. Draw a map that shows the way to a friend's house — or to a secret meeting place!

YOU WILL NEED
- Paper
- Colored pencils

1 Fold a sheet of paper twice (as shown). Make the bottom flap larger than the top two flaps.

2 Keep the paper folded while you draw a map on it. Draw the map right over the fold.

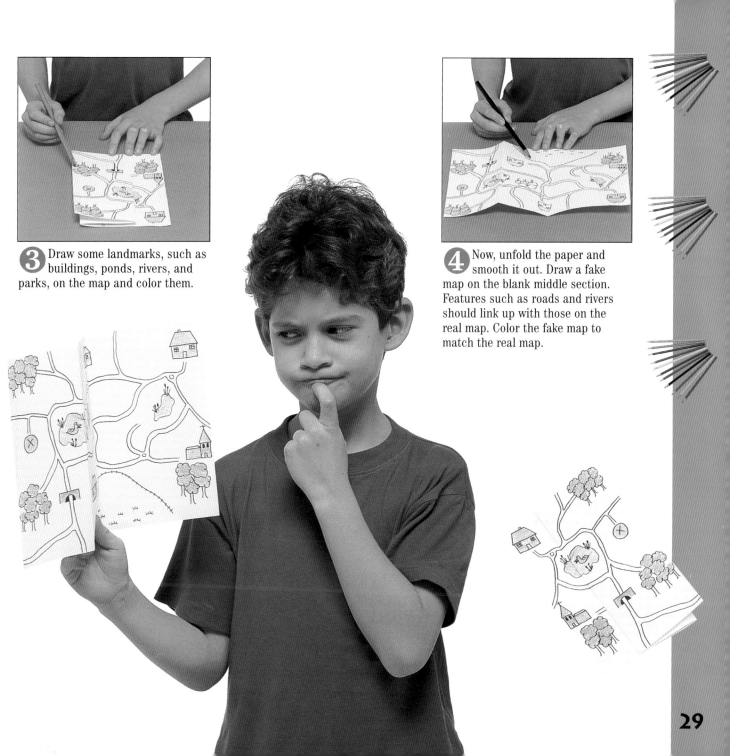

3 Draw some landmarks, such as buildings, ponds, rivers, and parks, on the map and color them.

4 Now, unfold the paper and smooth it out. Draw a fake map on the blank middle section. Features such as roads and rivers should link up with those on the real map. Color the fake map to match the real map.

Hidden Camera

Okay, Super Sleuth, you will need some photographs of your suspects. It is very important, of course, that you do not get caught taking pictures of them. What you need is a camera that is cleverly concealed inside an ordinary brown package.

1 Unfold a cardboard box. With the inside of the box facing up, place a camera, lens down, on one side. Keep the shutter release and the film advance lever near the edges. Trace around the lens and cut out an opening.

2 Put the camera back on the box, making sure the lens is over the cut opening. Use electrical tape to hold the camera securely in place, but do not tape over the shutter release or the film advance lever.

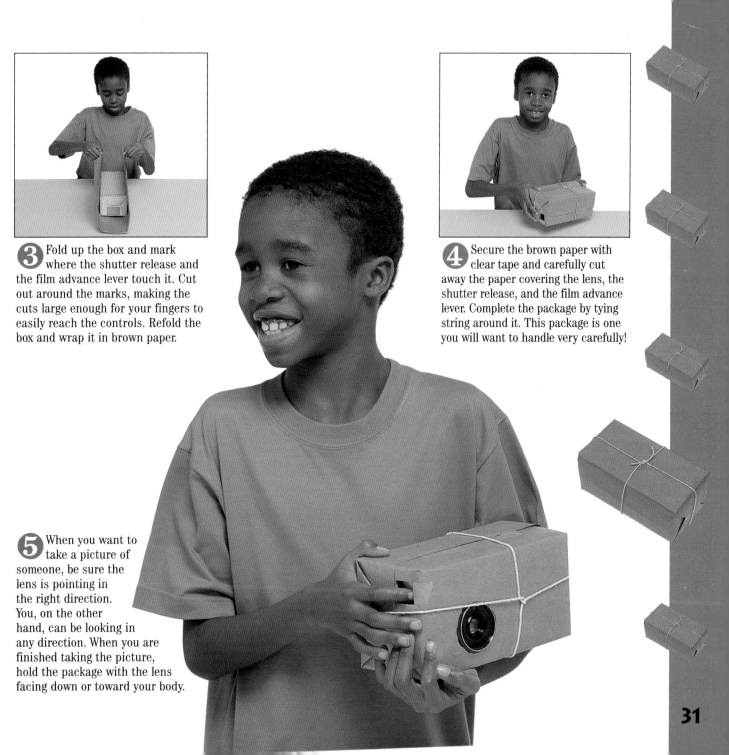

3 Fold up the box and mark where the shutter release and the film advance lever touch it. Cut out around the marks, making the cuts large enough for your fingers to easily reach the controls. Refold the box and wrap it in brown paper.

4 Secure the brown paper with clear tape and carefully cut away the paper covering the lens, the shutter release, and the film advance lever. Complete the package by tying string around it. This package is one you will want to handle very carefully!

5 When you want to take a picture of someone, be sure the lens is pointing in the right direction. You, on the other hand, can be looking in any direction. When you are finished taking the picture, hold the package with the lens facing down or toward your body.

Secret Pocket

Detectives often have to carry top secret documents. To prevent them from falling into the wrong hands, if they are searched, super sleuths hide the documents in a concealed pocket attached to the inside of their clothing. A secret pocket is easy to make and attach to a T-shirt. Just be careful with the safety pins!

YOU WILL NEED
- Scissors
- Ruler
- Felt
- Needle
- Thread
- Two safety pins
- T-shirt

1 Cut a rectangle, 11 inches (28 cm) by 5 inches (12.5 cm), out of felt. Make the rectangle smaller if you are hiding only small items. To make the pocket less noticeable, use felt that is the same color as the T-shirt.

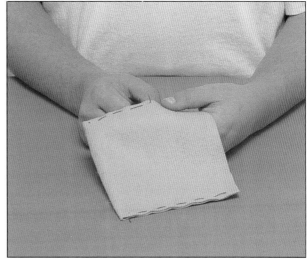

2 Fold the felt in half to make a square. Then, with a needle and thread, sew up both sides of the square to make a pocket. Do not sew across the top of the square. You might want to ask an adult to help you do the sewing.

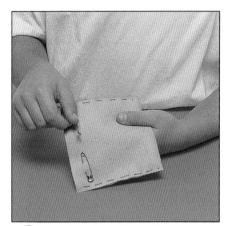

3 Attach safety pins, side by side, to one layer of felt near the opening of the pocket. Safety pins are sharp, so be careful not to prick yourself!

5 When no one is looking, quickly conceal your secret documents in the secret pocket. Do not hide bulky objects in this pocket — they will give the secret away. Before washing the T-shirt, remember to take the hidden documents out of the pocket.

4 Turn a T-shirt inside out, but remember which side is the front. Using the safety pins on the felt pocket, attach the pocket to the front of the T-shirt — on the inside. If you pin the pocket to the outside of the T-shirt, it will not be a secret!

Trick Wallet

When you open this wallet from one side, it looks empty, but when you open it the other way — wow! There is a secret document inside. Make two identical wallets so you and a fellow detective can exchange secret information without being detected. When you use the wallet to trick someone, distract the person so he or she does not notice you turning the wallet over.

1 Draw three rectangles, each 8 inches (20 cm) by 3 inches (7.5 cm), on a piece of cardboard and cut them out. To make a pocket-size version of this wallet, simply cut out three smaller rectangles.

2 Lay the rectangles side by side and attach them along the seams with electrical tape. The tape should act like a hinge, so the pieces of cardboard can fold over each other. Tape the seams on the back, too.

3 Attach electrical tape along each end, positioning the tape so it can be folded over onto the back. Trim off any excess tape.

4 Fold the wallet like an accordion (as shown). Then lay the wallet on a table and gently press it flat.

5 To test your trick wallet, place a small piece of cardboard, of a different color, between two of the flaps. Close the wallet and turn it over. If you do this correctly, the wallet will be empty when you open the flap.

6 Close the flap, turn the wallet over again, and open the flap. If all has gone according to plan, you will see the piece of cardboard you put into the wallet. Remember to turn the wallet over discreetly, so nobody catches on to the trick.

Double Envelope

To send secret documents by mail, all good detectives use a double envelope. This trick envelope has a hidden compartment only fellow detectives will know about. Anyone else opening the envelope will find it empty. If you really want to fool enemy agents, you can make up a false message and put it into the envelope.

YOU WILL NEED
- Scissors
- Two identical large envelopes
- Secret message
- Glue stick

1 Cut off the front of one envelope. Leave the flap attached but trim a little extra off the sides.

2 Slide the front of the cut envelope inside the other envelope. Make sure the flaps on both envelopes line up.

3 Place a secret message inside the envelope by sliding it between the cut piece of envelope and the front of the whole envelope.

4 Glue the two flaps of the envelopes together to seal the hidden compartment that now contains the secret message.

5 If the envelope falls into the wrong hands, it will look empty when it is opened — and the enemy will be very disappointed!

6 You and your friends will know exactly what to do with the trick envelope. Simply lift the glued flap and tear it off. Then slide your hand inside the hidden compartment and pull out the secret message.

Undercover Book

This clever piece of detective's equipment fools everyone! Although making an undercover book takes a little time and lots of patience, especially if you want a fairly deep hollow, it is definitely worth the effort. A large, thick book works best. If you cannot find a suitable, unwanted book at home, you can buy one very inexpensively at a secondhand bookstore.

YOU WILL NEED
- Unwanted hardcover book
- Pencil
- Ruler
- Scissors

1 Open the book at the front and turn over twenty pages. If the book is very thick, you can turn over more pages. Draw a rectangle on the right-hand page, leaving about a 1-inch (2.5-cm) border around the edges.

2 Cut out the rectangle. Then, using the hole as a stencil, draw a rectangle on the next right-hand page and cut it out. Repeat this step until the hollow is the right depth for the item you want to hide.

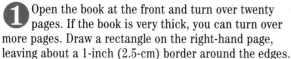

3 Do not cut through all the pages in the book; leave some pages at the back intact.

4 Place a secret item into the hollow and close the book. Put the undercover book on a shelf along with real books. No one will be able to tell the difference!

HANDY HINT

The undercover book can be used to hide many different things — candy, money, a code book, a diary, or even a tape of a secret conversation.

Candy Disguise

Everyone knows about sending messages in bottles, but only super sleuths know how to pass on vital pieces of information inside candy wrappers. The candy disguise does, however, pose one problem — resisting the temptation to eat the candy. If you eat the special piece of candy and throw away the wrapper, your message will remain a secret forever.

YOU WILL NEED
- Scissors
- Paper
- Pencil or pen
- Wrapped candies
- Clear tape
- Paper bag

1 Cut out a small rectangle of paper and write a secret message on it.

2 Unwrap one of the candies and place your message inside the wrapper.

3 Place the candy on top of the message and the wrapper and rewrap the candy.

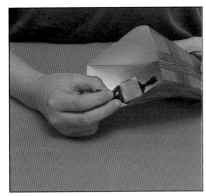

4 Make a loop out of a short piece of tape, with the sticky side of the tape on the outside of the loop. Stick the loop to the wrapper of the piece of candy with the message in it, then press that piece of candy against the inside of a paper bag, about halfway down.

6 To pass on the secret message to a friend, just empty the bag. The piece of candy with your message will remain stuck to the inside of the bag.

5 Fill the bag with the remaining candy. No one will suspect that you are carrying vital information inside a bag of candy.

7 Offer this piece of candy to your friend. He or she can eat it while reading the secret message.

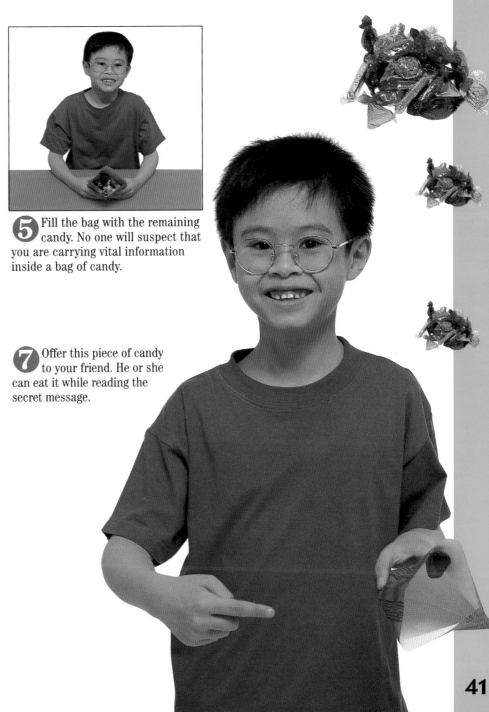

41

Handy Signals

Getting messages to other detectives can be tricky when you are involved in a hush-hush surveillance operation. So, instead of shouting messages, use hand signals. The next page shows you a handful of hand signals and their meanings. Use them alone to convey a simple message or link them together for more complicated instructions. When you have mastered these signals, go on to invent your own!

YOU WILL NEED
- Your hands

1 Press one finger over your lips when you want someone to stop talking. Move that finger over to your ear to say "listen."

2 Resting your chin on one hand with the thumb pointing up means "yes." To say "no," point your thumb down.

3 Position one hand loosely around your throat to warn fellow detectives about a dangerous situation.

4 Running your hand through your hair from the front to the back means "come here."

5 Hiding your face behind one hand means "go away." Use two hands to say "go away quickly."

6 Holding one finger next to your right eye means "look right," next to your left eye, "look left."

43

Flashing Messages

How can you send confidential messages over a long distance? Or at night? It is easy when you know how. All you need is a pocket-size mirror and a flashlight. Before you and other detectives go on a mission, however, you should agree on the meaning of each particular combination of flashes. It is a good idea to write your secret signals and their meanings in a code book.

YOU WILL NEED
- Flashlight
- Pocket-size mirror

1 A pocket-size mirror is a great signaling device for daytime use. Hold it so it catches the rays of the Sun, then jiggle it to flash a message.

2 Flashlights are particularly useful in the dark. Without them, you would just stumble around. Detectives also use flashlights to pinpoint their locations.

3 You can use the beam of a flashlight to spotlight a piece of evidence. To signal other detectives to move to a new position, flash the beam from left to right or right to left.

4 Detectives can send messages to each other at night by covering and uncovering the beam of a flashlight. Use three flashes to signal "danger" and one flash for "all clear." Special combinations of long and short flashes can be used for identification or to send more complicated messages.

HANDY HINT
When you are hiding from the enemy, you can signal your location to friends — without showing yourself — by flashing a secret code.

Mirror Vision

To be a successful detective, you have to learn all the tricks of the trade. The most important trick is knowing how to spy on people without getting caught. Here is where a pocket-size mirror comes in handy. Simply tape the mirror to a notebook so you can see what is going on behind you. Be warned, however, you might see something shocking!

YOU WILL NEED
- Clear tape
- Pocket-size mirror
- Spiral-bound notebook
- Juice box

1 Tape a pocket-size mirror to the front of a spiral-bound notebook. To hide the mirror, flip the back cover over the front of the book.

2 Hold the notebook as if you are reading something written on the page, but angle it so you can see what is going on behind you.

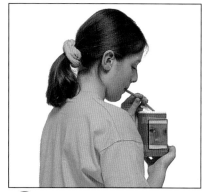

3 You can also tape the mirror to a juice box. As you sip the juice, angle the mirror to reflect the scene behind you.

HANDY HINT

Be careful using mirror vision. Flashes of sunlight bouncing off the mirror will give this surveillance trick away.

4 Hold a mirror in your hand and pretend to be removing a speck of dust from your eye. What you are really doing is taking a quick peek at what is happening behind you.

Invisible Writing

If you have not heard of invisible ink, you will probably be amazed by this piece of detective trickery. To write an invisible message, all you need is a lemon, a fine paintbrush, and a sheet of white paper. To read the invisible message, ask an adult to run a cool iron over the back of the paper.

YOU WILL NEED
- Knife
- Lemon
- Juicer
- Fine paintbrush
- White paper
- Iron

1 Ask an adult to cut a lemon in half. Place half of the lemon on a juicer. Push and turn the lemon to squeeze out the juice. Then squeeze the other half.

2 Dip a fine paintbrush into the lemon juice and write a coded message on a sheet of white paper. Let the paper dry thoroughly before giving it to a friend.

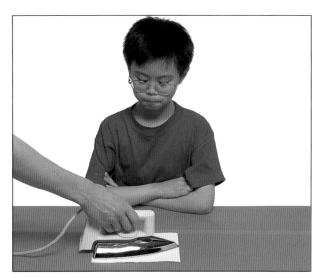

3 Now the magic happens! To read the secret message, your friend must ask an adult to iron the back of the sheet of paper. The iron should be set at its coolest temperature.

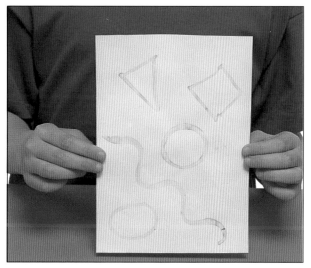

4 When your friend turns over the sheet of ironed paper, he or she will be able to see the message. The heat from the iron makes the message visible by turning the lemon juice light brown.

Intruder Detectors

A super sleuth is highly suspicious of everyone — especially family members who snoop around his or her bedroom or office uninvited. To catch these snoops, you can make two clever intruder detectors that are completely sneakproof and easy to install. These traps can be set on doors, windows, or drawers.

YOU WILL NEED
- Scissors
- Clear tape
- Cardboard

① **Intruder detector #1:** Use this trap to deal with someone very clever and observant. Even if the intruder suspects a trap, he or she will not spot this one. Cut a piece of clear tape 3½ inches (9 cm) long.

② Stick the piece of tape to a door, with half of the tape on the door and half of it on the door frame. Place the tape as close to the bottom of the door as possible. When the door is opened, the tape will come unstuck.

① **Intruder detector #2:** Although not as sneaky as the tape trap, this device is just as effective. Cut a small rectangle out of cardboard and fold it in half lengthwise. Use cardboard that is a color similar to the color of the door.

2 Insert the folded cardboard between the door and the door frame, just a short distance above the floor. Make sure the cardboard is firmly wedged. It should fall out only when the door is opened. If the cardboard keeps slipping out, it might be best to use the tape trap.

3 If the cardboard has fallen out, the trap has been sprung, and you know for certain that someone has been in your bedroom. What is a super sleuth's next move? Will you hunt down the intruder or set another trap?

Tricky Finger Pencil

All detectives need a finger pencil in their bag of tricks. This neat little device lets you write down notes about a suspect while you appear to be innocently reading a book. The final sneaky touch is to make the cover of your notebook look like a book jacket. The book should, of course, be a detective mystery!

YOU WILL NEED
- Pencil
- Ruler
- Pencil sharpener
- Scissors
- Cardboard
- Clear tape
- Notebook

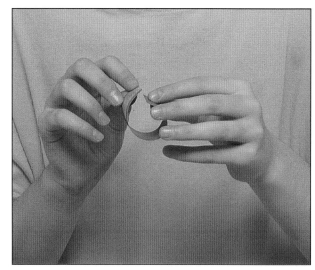

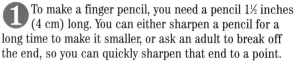 To make a finger pencil, you need a pencil 1½ inches (4 cm) long. You can either sharpen a pencil for a long time to make it smaller, or ask an adult to break off the end, so you can quickly sharpen that end to a point.

② Cut a piece of cardboard into a strip 2½ inches (6 cm) long and 1 inch (2.5 cm) wide. Wrap the strip around the top section of your thumb, adjusting the loop to fit your thumb. Then secure the seam with tape.

3 Place the pencil on the cardboard loop (as shown) and tape it into position. Be sure the pencil is attached securely so it does not move around when you are writing.

4 Place the cardboard loop over your thumb. Turn the loop until the pencil is in the correct position for writing — and make sure you are wearing the finger pencil on the correct hand! Now, hold your notebook in both hands (as shown) and practice using the pencil.

Electrical Trap

Making an electrical trap requires patience and a small amount of technical know-how. You will need an adult to help you with some parts of this project. All your efforts will be worth it, though, when the light goes on to warn you of an unwelcome guest.

YOU WILL NEED
- Scissors
- Cardboard
- Ruler
- Aluminum foil
- Clear tape
- Plastic-coated electrical wire (two colors)
- Small screwdriver
- Small flashlight bulb in a base
- Battery holder
- Two AA batteries

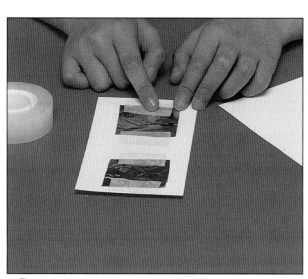

1 Cut a strip of cardboard 6½ inches (16.5 cm) by 4 inches (10 cm). Then cut out two squares of foil and tape them onto the cardboard. Fold the cardboard in half but do not let the foil squares touch each other.

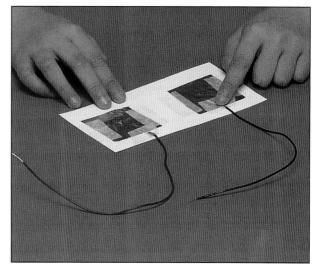

2 Ask an adult to cut two pieces of wire (as long as needed) and to strip the plastic coating off the ends of the wires. You will need lots of wire if the trap and the lightbulb are far apart. Tape a wire to each square of foil.

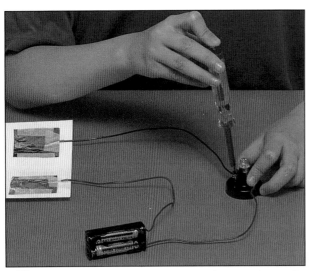

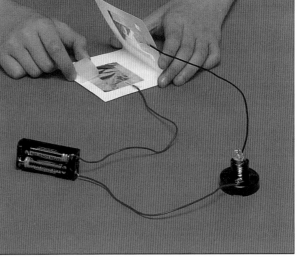

③ Use a screwdriver to connect one wire to the base of a flashlight bulb, the other to a battery holder. Have an adult cut another piece of wire and strip the ends. Attach one end to the lightbulb base, the other to the battery holder.

④ Make a loop of tape with the sticky surface on the outside. Press the loop onto one end of the cardboard strip. When someone steps on the trap, this loop of tape will keep the foil squares in contact, thereby completing an electrical circuit. When the squares of foil touch each other, the lightbulb goes on!

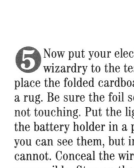

⑤ Now put your electrical wizardry to the test! Carefully place the folded cardboard under a rug. Be sure the foil squares are not touching. Put the lightbulb and the battery holder in a place where you can see them, but intruders cannot. Conceal the wires as much as possible. Step on the trap to make the foil squares touch each other. If the light goes on, your trap works!

Noisy Alarms

Crunch, crackle, pop, squeak! What are those noises? They are the sounds of your security alarms in action. Have you got some surprises for the next intruder!

1 **Noisy Alarm #1:** This alarm might sound a little odd, but crunchy cereal is great for nighttime security. Just leave a pile of cereal outside your bedroom door.

2 When an intruder accidentally steps on the cereal, you will hear CRUNCH, CRACKLE, POP! The intruder will know that he or she has been detected and will run away.

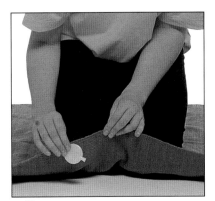

1 **Noisy Alarm #2:** Place one or two squeakers under a rug. When an intruder steps on the squeakers, you can catch the sneaky rascal.

2 In case the intruder misses the squeakers under the rug, hide another one under the cushion of a chair. Another good place to hide squeakers is under the bottom sheet of a bed.

Spotting an Impostor

You are going to meet an agent you have never seen before. You have no idea what he or she looks like, and there are no photographs in the files. How will you recognize the agent? How will you know the person you meet is not an impostor? Use one of these secret signals. They are quick and easy to prepare — and they are totally spyproof!

YOU WILL NEED
- Picture postcard
- Playing cards

1 **Secret Signal #1:** Tear a picture postcard in half and mail one of the halves to the person you are going to meet.

2 When you meet, you must each show your half of the postcard. If the other person's half does not match yours, he or she is an impostor.

1 **Secret Signal #2:** Telephone the person you are going to meet and agree to bring identical playing cards to the meeting.

2 When you meet, show each other the playing card you brought. Trust the person only if his or her card is the same as yours.

HANDY HINT

There are many different ways to identify a fellow detective or friendly agent. You can use a secret password or a secret handshake, or you can agree to be carrying a certain object. Keep changing your secret signals in case someone else learns about them.

A Final Challenge

This final challenge is the ultimate test of your skill and daring as a super sleuth. Your mission — if you accept it — is to remove a plastic bowling pin from a circle using only string, a rubber band, and an accomplice. Neither you nor your accomplice can enter the circle or touch the bowling pin with any parts of your bodies. The only part of the floor the bowling pin can touch is the area on which it is standing.

1 Use chalk to draw a circle with a 1-yard (1-meter) diameter. (A hoop is used in these photographs to show the circle more clearly.) Place a plastic bowling pin in the center of the circle. Now you really need a friend!

2 Cut four pieces of string, each 1½ yards (1½ m) long. Thread all four pieces of string through a single rubber band, with the rubber band halfway down each piece of string. Hold the ends of the strings (as shown).

3 Pull on the strings to stretch the rubber band so it will fit over the top of the bowling pin. Lower the rubber band carefully over the pin.

4 Relax your pull on the strings so the rubber band will tighten around the pin. Carefully raise the bowling pin out of the circle. Do not pull on the strings, or you will loosen the rubber band's grip on the pin.

Glossary

accomplice: a person who helps another person do something wrong or illegal.

ace: very good; of the highest quality.

agent: a person, such as a spy, who acts secretly or under cover for another person or group.

concealed: hidden or out of sight.

confidential: secret or private.

cover: (n) anything that hides, covers, or protects the safety or identity of a person or an object.

culprit: a person who has caused a problem or committed an illegal act.

detected: discovered or noticed, especially something hidden.

device: a tool or machine or piece of equipment designed for a specific use or purpose.

disguise: (n) clothing or make-up worn to hide the true identity of a person.

impostor: a person who pretends to be someone else in an attempt to trick or to cheat others.

intact: kept whole or unchanged.

intruder: a person who enters a place, often forcefully, without permission.

mystifying: mysteriously confusing or hard to figure out; puzzling.

observant: watchful; alert; aware of details.

physical evidence: items or objects that can be seen and touched, which provide clues to or facts about the truth of a situation.

resourceful: able to effectively solve problems or complete tasks in creative and clever ways.

shrewd: sharp; aware; clever in practical matters.

sleuth: a person who searches for information to solve a mystery; a detective or investigator.

snoop: (v) to look for information in a sneaky way.

stash: (v) to hide something or secretly put it away to keep it safe for future use.

surveillance: a close watch, sometimes secretly or under cover, over a person or a place to observe actions and events, such as a detective trailing a suspect.

suspect: (n) a person who might be guilty of doing something wrong or illegal.

talcum powder: powder that contains ground-up talc, which is a soft mineral with a soapy feel.

technical: related to mechanical, electrical, or some other kind of highly specialized knowledge or skill.

transformation: a change in the way a person or an object looks or acts so original characteristics no longer exist or cannot be recognized.

whisked: swept away with a quick, light motion.

More Books To Read

Crime and Detection. Brian Lane (Knopf)

Detective Dictionary: A Handbook for Aspiring Sleuths. Late-Night Library (series). Erich Ballinger (Lerner)

Detective Science: 40 Crime-Solving, Case-Breaking, Crook-Catching Activities for Kids. Jim Wiese (John Wiley & Sons)

Einstein Anderson, Science Detective: The Wings of Darkness. Seymour Simon (William Morrow & Company)

Fingerprints and Talking Bones: How Real-Life Crimes are Solved. Charlotte Foltz Jones (Bantam)

Secret Codes and Hidden Messages. Jeffrey A. O'Hare (Boyds Mills Press)

Spy. Richard Platt (Knopf)

Spy Science: 40 Secret-Sleuthing, Code-Cracking, Spy-Catching Activities for Kids. Jim Wiese (John Wiley & Sons)

Videos

Four Junior Detectives. (Vidmark)

Harriet the Spy. (Library Video)

Look What I Found: Making Codes and Solving Mysteries. (Library Video)

Sherlock Holmes: The Great Detective. (A & E)

Young Detectives on Wheels. (Films, Inc.)

Web Sites

www.discoverlearning.com/forensic/docs/index.html

www.fbi.gov/kids/kids.htm

Due to the dynamic nature of the Internet, some web sites stay current longer than others. To find additional web sites, use a reliable search engine with one or more of the following keywords: *crime, detective, espionage, forensic science, mystery, private investigator, secret agent, sleuth,* and *spy.*

Index